4/18

DUE

3-28-2022

Learning to Read, Step by Step!

Ready to Read   Preschool–Kinder
• big type and easy words • rhyme and rhyt
For children who know the alphabet and
begin reading.

Reading with Help   Preschool–Gr
• basic vocabulary • short sentences • simp
For children who recognize familiar wo
new words with help.

Reading on Your Own   Grades 1-
• engaging characters • easy-to-follow plo
For children who are ready to read on t

Reading Paragraphs   Grades 2–
• challenging vocabulary • short paragrapl
For newly independent readers who re
with confidence.

Ready for Chapters   Grades 2–4
• chapters • longer paragraphs • full-color
For children who want to take the plunge into chapter books
but still like colorful pictures.

Cat. No. 23-221

STEP INTO READING® is designed to give every child a successful
reading experience. The grade levels are only guides; children will progress
through the steps at their own speed, developing confidence in their reading.
The F&P Text Level on the back cover serves as another tool to help you
choose the right book for your child.

Remember, a lifetime love of reading starts with a single step!

In memory of Beatrice,
my favorite chicken
—S.H.

Text copyright © 2013 by Sandra Horning
Interior illustrations copyright © 2013 by Jon Goodell
Cover photograph copyright © Arterra Picture Library/Alamy

Visit us on the Web!
StepIntoReading.com
randomhousekids.com

Educators and librarians, for a variety of teaching tools, visit us at
RHTeachersLibrarians.com

Library of Congress Cataloging-in-Publication Data
Horning, Sandra.
Chicks! / by Sandra Horning ; illustrated by Jon Goodell.
    p.   cm. — (Step into Reading. Step 1)
Summary: A family learns about raising chickens when they buy baby chicks from a local farm.
ISBN 978-0-307-93221-1 (trade) — ISBN 978-0-375-97117-4 (lib. bdg.) —
ISBN 978-0-375-98114-2 (ebook)
[1. Chickens—Fiction. 2. Animals—Infancy—Fiction.] I. Goodell, Jon, ill. II. Title.
PZ7.H7867Ch 2013
[E]—dc23   2011050438

Printed in the United States of America
10 9 8 7 6 5 4 3

This book has been officially leveled by using the F&P Text Level Gradient™ Leveling System.

Chicks!

by Sandra Horning

illustrations by Jon Goodell

Random House 🏠 New York

We drive to a farm.

We buy chicks.

The chicks go
for a car ride.

Soon we are home.

The chicks are
small and soft.

They chirp and chirp.

We put the chicks
in a brooder.

They need water and
food in their new home.

The brooder has a light.
The light keeps the
chicks warm.

The chicks grow . . .

. . . and grow.

They grow
new feathers.

The chicks can fly
out of the brooder.

We build a coop outside.

The chicks move in.

They grow some more.

The chicks
grow combs
and wattles.

Their beaks
grow bigger.

Their feathers
grow fuller.

Now they are chickens.

We build nest boxes.

The chickens
cluck and cluck.

Some of the
chickens lay eggs.

treating

abused

adolescents

eliana gil